Treasure Island

ROBERT LOUIS STEVENSON

ADAPTED BY

Janice Greene

SADDLEBACK PUBLISHING, INC.

SADDLEBACK *Classics*

The Call of the Wild
A Christmas Carol
Frankenstein
The Adventures of Huckleberry Finn
The Red Badge of Courage
The Scarlet Letter
A Tale of Two Cities
Treasure Island

Development and Production: Laurel Associates, Inc.
Cover and Interior Art: Black Eagle Productions

SADDLEBACK PUBLISHING, INC.
3505 Cadillac Ave., Building F-9
Costa Mesa, CA 92626-1443

ISBN 1-56254-281-8

Printed in the United States of America
05 04 03 02 01 00 M 99   9 8 7 6 5 4 3 2 1

CONTENTS

§1 The End of Billy Bones

Squire Trelawney and some of the other gentlemen have asked me to write down the story of Treasure Island. I, Jim Hawkins, gave them my promise to do so. So I will tell you everything that happened—from beginning to end. I will leave out nothing except the location of the island—for there is still treasure there.

I go back in time to the year 17__. This is when my father still ran the Admiral Benbow Inn. And this is the same year the old sailor came into the inn, carrying a battered old sea chest.

He was a tall, rough-looking man, brown as a nut. His hands were scarred. Across one cheek was a jagged old scar from the slash of a sword.

"Do many people come this way?" he asked.

My father said, "No, very few."

That was true. We lived on a lonely stretch of the English coast. Few travelers came our way.

One day, the old seaman took me aside. He promised to pay me a silver coin every month if I would keep an eye out for "a man with one leg." I was to tell him at once if I saw such a man.

People were afraid of the old seaman, whom my family now called Captain. At night, he would drink far more rum than his head could carry. Then he would sing wicked songs that made the house shake.

His bloodthirsty stories frightened everyone. My father said the Captain was ruining business at the inn.

And in one way, he did ruin us. Month after month he stayed—without paying my father a penny. I am sure the trouble and worry over this man caused the sickness that befell my poor father. In the days that followed, we paid little notice to the Captain. My father was getting worse, and my mother and I were busy with the inn.

One cold morning when the Captain was away, a stranger came to the inn. He was a pale man, with two fingers missing on his left hand. He wore a cutlass.

He said he was looking for a man with a scar on his cheek.

I told him the Captain had gone out walking, but would return soon.

An hour or so later, he walked in the door.

The stranger said, "Bill."

The Captain turned. He had the look of a man who sees a ghost. He cried out, "Black Dog!"

Black Dog said, "Yes, it's Black Dog—come to see his old shipmate, Billy Bones. We'll sit down now, if you please, and talk square."

Black Dog sent me to fetch some rum. Then he told me to leave the room. Their voices grew louder and louder. Then all of a sudden an explosion of swearing erupted. I heard a chair and table tumble over. Then a clash of steel and a cry of pain. The next instant, Black Dog came running out, with the Captain right behind him. Blood was running from his shoulder.

Just at the door of the inn, the Captain made a great swing with his cutlass. Such a blow might have split Black Dog to his chin! Instead, the cutlass hit the wooden sign that said "Admiral Benbow" and cut a notch in it.

The Captain reeled and leaned against the wall unsteadily.

I cried, "Are you hurt?"

"Rum!" he cried. "Bring me rum, Jim!"

When I returned with the rum, the Captain was lying on the floor. His breath was loud and hard. His eyes were shut and his face was a horrible color. My mother and I did not know what to do.

Luckily, Dr. Livesey came by to visit my father just then. We were glad to see him.

Dr. Livesey turned up Bill's sleeve. We saw that one of his tattoos read "Billy Bones." So that was his name!

Dr. Livesey cut open a vein. He bled Billy Bones a long time before the man opened his eyes.

"Where's Black Dog?" he asked.

Dr. Livesey said, "There is no Black Dog

here—except what you have on your own back. You've been drinking so much rum you've had a stroke, just as I warned you. If you keep on drinking, you'll have another, and that will be the end of you."

Later, I took some medicines to Bones, who was lying in bed.

"Did that doctor say how long I was to lie here?" he asked.

"A week at least," I answered.

Bones said, "Thunder! I can't do that. They'll have the Black Spot on me by then. It's my sea chest they're after. If they come, you get on a horse and go—go to that doctor. Tell him to get all hands—magistrates and such. They can round up Captain Flint's old crew—all that's left of 'em. I was old Flint's first mate. I'm the only one who knows where the map is. Flint gave it to me at Savannah, when he lay a-dying."

Then Bones fell into a heavy sleep. I should have told the doctor what he said—all about his sea chest, and the crew from Captain Flint's ship who might come after it. But my poor father died quite suddenly that evening. I had little time to think about Billy Bones. Though he seemed to grow weaker, he helped himself to rum from the bar. We did not dare try to stop him.

The day after the funeral, I was standing at the door of the inn. I was full of sad thoughts about my father. Then I noticed a blind man coming up the road. He tapped a stick in front of his feet. His back was hunched and he wore a huge, ragged cloak.

He stopped in front of the inn and said softly, "Will any kind friend tell this poor blind man where he is?"

I said, "Yes, sir. You are at the Admiral Benbow Inn."

"Will you give me your hand, my kind young friend, and lead me in?" he asked.

But when I held out my hand, he grabbed it in a grip as strong as a vise! I tried to pull away from him.

Suddenly his voice turned cruel and cold. He said, "Take me to Billy Bones. *Now*, boy—or I'll break your arm!"

I took him into Bones's room. Billy took one look at the blind man. The rum seemed to go out of him in an instant. He tried to get up, but he could not.

The blind man said, "Now, Billy Bones— stay where you are. Hold out your left hand."

Then he turned to me. He said, "Boy, take his left hand by the wrist. Bring it near to my right."

I obeyed him. Then I saw the blind man put something in the Captain's hand.

The blind man said, "Now, that's done." Then suddenly he let go of me and hurried out of the inn without any help. I could hear his stick tap-tap-tapping into the distance.

Billy looked at his hand. He cried, "Ten o'clock! I have just six hours."

He sprang to his feet. Then he put his hand to his throat, made a strange sound, and fell with a crash to the floor.

I ran to him and called to my mother. But there was no need to hurry. Billy was dead. I had never liked the man, although I had begun to pity him. But when I saw he was dead, I burst out in a flood of tears. It was the second death I had known. The sadness of the first still filled my heart.

§ 2 Flint's Treasure Map

Flint's men would be back in six hours! My mother and I were in a dangerous spot. We ran to the village for help. But no one in the village would help us. The name of Captain Flint meant nothing to me, but it filled the townspeople with fear.

My mother was determined to go back to the inn. She needed the money Billy Bones owed her. She said to all of the villagers, "Jim and I will go back alone. Small thanks to you—you chicken-hearted men! We'll have that sea chest open if we die for it."

Even then no man would go with us. All they would do was give me a loaded pistol. They also sent one man to ride for help.

Back at the inn, my mother whispered, "Draw down the blinds, Jim. Flint's men might come and watch from outside."

I bent over Billy Bones's body. On the floor close to his hand there was a round bit of paper. On one side was written, "You have until ten tonight." The other side was black. *It was the Black Spot!*

We found a key on a string around the Captain's neck. In a twinkling, my mother opened the chest.

Inside was a suit of good clothes, never worn. There were also some sticks of tobacco, two fine pistols, a piece of silver, an old Spanish watch, and five or six curious shells. Beneath those things we found an old cloak, a bundle that looked like papers tied up in oilskin, and a small canvas bag. The bag gave a jingle of gold.

My mother said, "I'll show these scoundrels I'm an honest woman. Give me the bag, Jim. I'll take what Billy Bones owed me, and not a penny more."

Counting out the money was a difficult business, for the coins were from many countries. When we were about half finished, I heard a sound that brought my

heart into my mouth. It was the tap-tap-tapping of the blind man's stick! After that, we heard a low whistle from off on the hill.

I said, "Mother, take *all* the money and let's be going!"

My mother said, "I'll take just what I've counted out."

"Then I'll take this to make it up," I said, snatching the oilskin bundle. We then started to run toward the village.

Behind us, we could hear thundering footsteps. Suddenly my mother cried, "My dear, take the money and run on. I fear I am going to faint." Luckily, we were only a short way from the inn, near a little bridge. I led her under the arch where we both hid.

Seven or eight men came running up to the inn. I heard the voice of the blind man crying out, "Get inside! In, in, in!"

The men rushed inside. Then one of them called out, "Bones is dead!"

The blind man swore. "Search him! Get into his sea chest!"

A few minutes later one of the men called out to the blind man, "Pew, they've been here before us! They've gone through the chest! Only the money's left!"

Pew roared, "It's that *boy*! I wish I had put his eyes out! Scatter, men—we must find him immediately!"

The men ran through the inn, throwing furniture over and kicking in the doors with their heavy boots. Then came a whistle.

One of the men said, "There's the signal again. We've got to go, mates!"

Pew cried, "Never mind that, you fools! You'll have your hands on *thousands* if you can find it! Oh, shiver my soul, if only I had eyes!" He began to swing his stick at the men, right and left. He hit more than one of them. They swore and tried to grab the stick from Pew's hands.

Then from the top of the hill came the sound of galloping horses. The men ran away in every direction. Pew was left alone. In a frenzy he went tapping up and down the road calling, "Mates! You wouldn't leave old Pew! Not old Pew!"

Just then the horses swept down the hill toward the inn. Pew ran straight for the ditch and fell in. He was on his feet in a second. Then he made another dash—right into a huge, galloping horse!

The rider could not stop in time. Down went Pew with a cry that rang into the night. He fell on his face and moved no more.

The riders were revenue officers. They went back to the inn with my mother and me. The place was in a state of ruin.

One officer asked me, "Do you know what they were after?"

I said, "I think I have the thing in my

pocket. I thought perhaps, Dr. Livesey—"

The officer said, "Perfectly right. Dr. Livesey is a gentleman and a magistrate. I'll make my report out to him and I'll take you along, Jim Hawkins."

We found Dr. Livesey at the Hall, where Squire Trelawney lived. Squire Trelawney was a tall, broad man, with a face made rough and red by his long travels. His eyebrows were thick and black, and he had a quick, high temper.

I told Squire Trelawney and Dr. Livesey what had happened. When the name of Captain Flint was mentioned, Squire Trelawney became very excited. He said, "Why, old Captain Flint was the most bloodthirsty buccaneer who ever lived! The Spanish were so afraid of Flint I was sometimes *proud* he was an Englishman! If I had a clue where his treasure was, I'd search for a year to find it."

After giving me a hearty supper of pigeon pie, Dr. Livesey carefully opened the oilskin packet. Inside was the map of an island, showing latitude and longitude. There was a hill named "Spyglass" and a cross. Beneath the cross was written *treasure*.

The squire said, "*Treasure*, Livesey! Tomorrow I will leave for Bristol. In three weeks—no, two weeks—no—in ten days— we'll have the best crew in England! Young Jim Hawkins here will be cabin boy. You, Livesey, are ship's doctor. I am admiral. We'll take my servants: Redruth, Joyce, and Hunter. With luck we'll have good winds and a quick journey. I trust we'll have no trouble in finding the spot. Then we'll have money to eat! Money enough to roll in!"

Dr. Livesey said, "All right, Trelawney, I'll go with you—and so will Jim Hawkins. There's only one man I'm afraid of."

Squire Trelawney said, "*Who?*"

"You—for you cannot hold your tongue," Dr. Livesey said. "We are not the only men who know of this paper. The men who attacked the inn tonight are not far off."

Squire Trelawney said, "Livesey, you are always right. I'll be as silent as the grave."

§3 Long John Silver

Several weeks later, Squire Trelawney wrote a letter from Bristol. He had bought a fine ship named *Hispaniola*. At first the squire had trouble finding a crew. But a stroke of luck had brought him an old, one-legged sailor named Long John Silver. The squire hired him to be the ship's cook. Long John Silver said he knew many sailors, so he helped Squire Trelawney find the rest of the crew.

Squire Trelawney had paid to repair the broken furniture at the inn. He had even added some new furniture, and a beautiful armchair for my mother. The squire also found a boy to help her while I was away. I spent one last night at the inn before I took the coach for Bristol with Squire Trelawney's servant, Redruth.

In Bristol, Squire Trelawney sent me to take a note to Long John Silver. I went to a tavern called "Spyglass."

As I stood at the door of the tavern, I saw the man I knew must be Long John Silver. His left leg was cut off close to the hip. Under his left shoulder he carried a crutch. He hopped about on it as easily as a bird. The man was very tall and strong, with a face as big as a ham. His face was plain and pale, but intelligent and friendly looking.

When I had first heard about Long John Silver, I was afraid he might be the one-legged man Billy Bones had been waiting for. But one look at him told me I must be wrong. This clean and smiling man was nothing like Billy Bones, or Black Dog, or Pew—or any of the others.

I called to him, "Mr. Silver, sir?"

Long John Silver took the note. He said. "Ah, you are our new cabin boy! I am pleased to see you." He shook my hand.

Just then one of the men in the tavern got up suddenly and rushed for the door.

I cried, "Oh, stop him! It's Black Dog!"

Long John Silver cried, "I don't care who he is. He hasn't paid. Stop him!"

The man who was closest to the door ran after Black Dog, but came back alone.

Seeing Black Dog in Long John Silver's tavern had made me suspicious. But Long John Silver insisted he had never seen the man before. I didn't see that Long John Silver was too deep and too clever for me.

Later that day, Squire Trelawney took me on board the *Hispaniola*. It was there that I first met Captain Smollett. He was a serious, sharp-eyed man. He seemed angry with everything on the ship. When we were in the cabin with Dr. Livesey, Captain Smollett came in and shut the door behind him.

Frowning, Smollett looked the squire in the eye. He said, "I better speak plain, sir. I don't like your plans, and I don't like the men on this ship."

Dr. Livesey said, "What? Why don't you like the plans?"

Captain Smollett said, "I don't like treasure voyages. And I especially don't like them when they're secret—and everyone knows the secret. There's been too much blabbing."

Squire Trelawney looked annoyed. "I never told that to a soul!" he cried.

Smollett went on. "The crew knows it. They know where the island is. They also know you have a map that shows where the treasure is buried."

"Now tell us why you don't like the crew," Dr. Livesey said.

Captain Smollett said, "I don't, sir— though there's nothing I can prove against them. But I will tell you what I want—I want the guns and gunpowder kept safe under this cabin. And no more loose talk."

Dr. Livesey said, "In other words, Captain, you fear a mutiny."

Unhappily, Squire Trelawney said, "I will do as you ask, Captain Smollett. But I must say I think the worse of you."

"As you please, sir," said Smollett. "You'll find that I do my duty."

And he went out of the cabin.

Dr. Livesey said, "I think you have hired two honest men for this crew—Captain

Smollett and Long John Silver."

Squire Trelawney said, "Well, Long John Silver is honest."

Dr. Livesey said, "We shall see."

All that night we were busy loading the boat. I was tired as a dog before morning came, but I was much too excited to sleep. Finally, all the supplies were loaded onto the *Hispaniola*. Long John Silver led the crew in song:

"Fifteen men on the dead man's chest—
Yo-ho-ho, and a bottle of rum!"

Then at last the anchor was brought up and the sails began to puff out in the wind. Finally—the *Hispaniola* was on her way to Treasure Island!

I am not going to tell much about the trip itself. It was mostly pleasant. All the crew liked and respected Long John Silver. To me, he was always kind. I liked to visit him in the galley. He kept it as clean as a new pin. The dishes were hung up, shined and bright. In the corner of the galley, his parrot would call out from his cage, "Pieces of eight! Pieces of eight! Pieces of eight!"

Squire Trelawney and Captain Smollett had little to say to each other. But the squire was very generous with the crew. If he heard it was a man's birthday, he would put out a large barrel of apples.

One night when my work was over, I came to get an apple before going to bed. I climbed into the barrel, for there were only a few left at the bottom. For a moment I sat there in the dark, while the ship rocked me. I was about to fall asleep when I heard Long John Silver's voice. As soon as he started to speak, I began to tremble. It was clear that the lives of every honest man on the ship depended on me!

Long John Silver said, "Flint was the captain, and I was one of his crew. That's when I lost my leg, and old Pew lost his eyes. There was plenty of money I got for that trip. But after this trip, I'll be set up as a real gentleman. What do you say, mate? Are you with me?"

One man shouted, "I'm with you!"

Then another man spoke up. "What I

want to know is—just how long must we wait around? I've had almost enough of Captain Smollett, I tell you."

Long John Silver said, "You'll wait until *I* give the word! Captain Smollett's a first-rate seaman. And Squire Trelawney and Dr. Livesey have the map of the island. I mean to have them help *us* find the treasure. Then we'll strike!"

One man cried out, "You're a clever one, Long John Silver!"

With an evil grin, Long John Silver said, "There's only one man I claim. I claim Squire Trelawney. I swear I'll wring his head off his body with these hands!"

Just then a sort of brightness fell upon me in the barrel. Looking up, I saw the moon had risen. Almost at the same time, the lookout shouted, "Land ho!"

There was a great rush of feet across the deck. I made sure no one was watching before I climbed out of the barrel.

Very early the next morning, I asked Dr. Livesey if I could see him and Squire Trelawney and Captain Smollett alone.

When we were gathered in the cabin, I told them what I had heard.

Captain Smollett said, "We have some time before us—at least until this treasure is found. Now, which men can we count on? Squire Trelawney, can we count on your servants to be on our side?"

"Yes," Squire Trelawney said.

Captain Smollett said, "That makes three. Counting the four of us, that makes seven. The others—we don't know."

Dr. Livesey said, "Jim can help us. The men are not shy around him. He might overhear more of their plans."

Squire Trelawney said, "Jim Hawkins, I'm putting my faith in you."

I began to feel pretty desperate. We could make all the plans we liked—but there were only seven of us, and 19 of them!

§ 4 On Treasure Island

By morning we were close to Treasure Island. The wind had almost stopped, and the still air was very hot. The crew sweated and swore at their work.

As we came close to shore there was a strange smell in the air. I thought it seemed like wet leaves and rotting tree trunks. Dr. Livesey sniffed the air as if he were tasting a bad egg. He said, "I don't know about treasure, but I'll bet my wig there's *fever* on this island!"

The tempers of the crew got worse. They answered every order with a black look. The threat of mutiny hung over us like a thundercloud. Only Long John Silver was in good spirits. If he was given an order, he would call out, "aye, aye, sir!" in a cheerful voice, hopping off on his crutch in an instant. It seemed he was trying to hide the dark mood of the rest of the crew.

We had a quick meeting in the cabin. Captain Smollett said, "If I give another order we'll have mutiny on our hands. There's only one man we can count on."

"Who is that?" asked the squire.

Captain Smollett said, "Long John Silver. He doesn't want a mutiny now. Let's give the crew a free afternoon on the island. I promise that Silver will bring them back on board as mild as lambs."

And so it was decided. The four of us took loaded pistols. Squire Trelawney's servants, Hunter, Joyce, and Redruth, were given pistols, too.

Captain Smollett then told the crew they could have a free afternoon on the island. They gave a roaring cheer that set a cloud of birds flying around the ship.

The crew began loading themselves into boats. Suddenly I had a wild idea that later helped to save our lives. I decided to go onto the island myself! I slipped over the side and hid in the front of the nearest boat.

When we were close to the trees on shore, I caught a branch and swung myself out of the boat. I ran into the trees. Behind me, I heard Long John Silver call, "Jim! Jim!" But I ran on and on, until I could run no longer.

All at once there was movement in front of me. A duck flew up with a quack, then another and another. Soon clouds of birds were screaming and circling in the air. I heard voices. One of them was that of Long John Silver!

At first I hid under a fallen oak tree. But I knew I must get close to Silver if I wanted to hear. If I had been such a fool as to come onto the island, the least I could do was to listen to the crew's plans.

I crawled closer. Long John Silver was talking to one of the crew. He said, "I'm warning you, Tom—because I want to save your neck. If you're not with us, you're against us!"

In a shaking voice, Tom said, "I won't get mixed up in this, Long John Silver! I won't turn against my duty. I'd rather lose my hand!"

Suddenly, far away from us, there came a great cry of anger. Then, one long, horrid scream rang out.

Tom leaped at the sound. Long John Silver didn't bat an eye. Like a snake about to spring, he watched Tom.

Tom cried, "What was that?"

Long John Silver's eyes shone like crumbs of glittering glass. He said, "*That?* Oh, I think that must have been Alan."

Tom said, "*Alan!* Then rest his soul for a true seaman. And as for you, Long John

Silver—you're a mate of mine no longer. You've killed Alan, have you? Then kill me too, if you can."

With that, Tom bravely turned his back on Long John Silver and walked away.

Crying out, Long John Silver grabbed onto a tree branch. Then he whipped his crutch from under his arm and sent it flying through the air. It hit poor Tom in the back. The man gasped and fell.

In an instant, Long John Silver was on him. He stabbed him twice with his knife.

For a few moments, the world whirled before my eyes. When my senses cleared, I saw Tom lying dead on the ground. Long John Silver was cleaning his knife in the grass. Everything else was exactly the same—as if nothing had happend. The sun was still shining. I could hardly believe that murder had actually been done!

Long John Silver took out a whistle and blew it several times. I crawled to an open space. Then I began to run and run. It was all over for me, I thought. Either the crew would find me and kill me, or I would starve.

I ran on until I was at the foot of a little hill. Here I saw something dark and shaggy leaping from behind the trunk of a tree! I turned and ran, but, moving very quickly, it cut me off. Seeing that the thing was a man, I was very frightened. Then I remembered I had a pistol. I walked closer and saw he was a white man, like myself. His skin was burnt dark by the sun. His clothes were rags, held together with buttons and bits of stick.

I asked, "Who are you?"

"I'm poor Ben Gunn, I am," he croaked. "I haven't spoken to a soul for three years. I was *marooned*, mate! I've lived on goats and berries and oysters. Now you—what do you call yourself?"

"Jim," I answered.

Ben Gunn said, "*Jim!* Ah, Jim, you'll bless your stars, you will. For you were the first that found me! I'm rich! Rich!"

I thought the poor fellow must have gone crazy from being alone so long.

Then Ben Gunn asked, "Now, Jim, you tell me true—is that Captain Flint's ship?"

I said, "It's not Flint's ship. Flint is dead.

But some of Flint's men are on board. Worse luck for the rest of us."

Ben Gunn gasped. "Not Long John Silver! If you were sent by Long John Silver, I'm as good as dead."

I began to think Ben Gunn might help us. I told him the whole story of our trip, and all about the trouble we were in.

Ben Gunn said, "You put your trust in me. I were in Flint's ship. Billy Bones were there and so were Long John Silver. We waited with the ship, the *Walrus*, while Flint went off to bury the treasure. He had six men with him—six strong seamen. When he came back, all six were killed. How he done it, we never knew. We asked him where the treasure was hid. But all he said was, 'You can stay if you like. This ship's going after more treasure!'"

Ben Gunn went on. "Well, three years ago, I was on another ship. When we spotted the island I said, 'Here's Flint's treasure, boys. Let's land and find it.' Twelve days we looked for it. And every day the men had a worse word for me. Then one fine morning, they all went aboard. 'Here's a shovel, a pick, and a rifle,' they said. 'You can stay here on Treasure Island and find Flint's money for yourself.'"

Then Ben Gunn winked and gave me a pinch. He said, "Now this Squire Trelawney. If a man was to help him out, would the squire be a generous man?"

I said that indeed Squire Trelawney was a most generous man.

Ben Gunn said, "And would this Squire Trelawney let the man who helped him sail home on the *Hispaniola*?"

I said, "Why, Squire Trelawney is a gentleman. And besides, if we got rid of the others, we would need your help getting the *Hispaniola* back home."

Ben Gunn said, "Well, Jim, there's a boat I made with my own two hands. I keep her under that white rock over there."

Just then the loud boom of a cannon thundered in the distance.

I cried, "The fight is on! Follow me!"

§5 Defending the Stockade

On the *Hispaniola*, Dr. Livesey, Squire Trelawney, and Captain Smollett made plans. Most of the mutineers had left for the island. Only six men were still on board. At first Dr. Livesey and the others thought they might attack those men and then sail away. But there was not a breath of wind. Then the squire's servant, Hunter, gave the news that I had gone onto the island. Knowing what a dangerous mood the mutineers were in, they feared for my life.

Dr. Livesey decided to take Hunter and row over to Treasure Island. He had seen a stockade on Billy Bones's map of the island. He wanted to see what sort of a place it was.

They discovered the stockade was on a hill, and well built. Inside stood a strong house made of logs. Best of all, there was a spring of clean, clear water there. This made the stockade a better place to fight the mutineers than on the ship. There was no more water on board the *Hispaniola*.

Dr. Livesey and Hunter went back to the ship. The doctor told the others about the stockade. He gave Redruth three loaded muskets to guard the cabin. Then they loaded the little boat with gunpowder, muskets, bags of biscuits, small barrels of pork, and Dr. Livesey's medicine chest.

Before leaving, Captain Smollett called to the six men on the *Hispaniola*. He said, "We have our pistols ready. If any one of you makes a signal to the men on the island, that man's dead."

They rowed back to Treasure Island and carried the food and weapons into the log house. Joyce, with half a dozen muskets, was left behind to stand guard. Then they rowed back to the *Hispaniola* for another load.

They quickly loaded the boat with more food. Then Captain Smollett called out to one of the six men on board. "Hear me, Abraham Gray! I am leaving this ship. I know you are a good man at heart. I have my watch in my hand. I give you 30 seconds to join me."

There was silence. Then came the sound of a sudden scuffle and out burst Abraham Gray with a knife cut on the side of his cheek! He ran to his captain like a dog to the whistle.

Abraham Gray said, "I'm with you, sir."

In a moment the small boat was rowing toward Treasure Island.

Suddenly Captain Smollett cried out, "The cannon!"

They looked back toward the *Hispaniola*. As they watched in horror, they saw the five men left on board getting the cannon ready to fire. One of the men, Israel Hands, was lifting a cannonball.

Gray said, "Israel was the gunner on Flint's ship."

"Who's the best shot here?" Smollett asked.

Dr. Livesey said, "Trelawney, by far."

Squire Trelawney was as cool as steel. He got his gun ready.

Captain Smollett said, "Now, easy with that gun, sir, or you'll swamp the boat."

Squire Trelawney aimed his musket at Israel Hands and fired. But just as he fired, Israel bent down. The musket ball whistled over him, and another man fell to the deck.

The mutineers on shore heard the shot. They ran out of the trees toward their boats.

Dr. Livesey cried out, "They're coming for us!"

"They'll have a hard time catching us," Smollett said. "It's not *them* I fear—it's the cannon. My lady's maid couldn't miss this boat!"

The little boat was now close to shore. But the tide was carrying it away from the mutineers on the island. The greatest danger was indeed the cannon.

Squire Trelawney aimed his gun once more. But just then the *Hispaniola*'s cannon fired. Captain Smollett and Redruth leaned backward. A wall of water washed over the boat, but the cannon shot seemed to go over the men's heads.

The boat gently sank in shallow water.

No one was hurt, but the food and most of the guns were lost. Dr. Livesey and the others waded to shore with all due speed. Through the trees, they could hear the voices of the mutineers.

The men hurried as fast as they could toward the stockade. With every step, the shouts of the mutineers seemed closer. The squire's gun had been lost when the boat sank, so Captain Smollett gave him his own gun. Dr. Livesey gave his cutlass to Gray, who spit on his hand, grabbed the cutlass and made it sing through the air. It did the other men's hearts good to see him so ready to fight his former mates.

Just then, the mutineers burst out of the trees. When Squire Trelawney fired, one of the mutineers fell to the ground, dead. The rest turned and ran off.

Just then, a pistol cracked in the bushes. Poor Redruth stumbled and fell. Dr. Livesey and Squire Trelawney fired back, but there was nothing to shoot at. All was suddenly quiet. It seemed the mutineers had disappeared.

Dr. Livesey looked at Redruth. It was clear he had not long to live. The men carried him through the gates of the stockade and into the log house.

Squire Trelawney dropped down on his knees beside Redruth. Crying like a child, he kissed his servant's hand.

Redruth asked, "Am I going, doctor?"

Dr. Livesey said, "Yes, my good man, you're going home."

One of the men read a prayer. A little while later, Redruth passed away.

While on the *Hispaniola*, Captain Smollett had tucked several things in his chest and pockets—a British flag, a rope, a Bible, and some tobacco. He and Hunter flew the flag from a tall tree.

Captain Smollett said, "It's a pity we lost that second load. We still have plenty of gunpowder and shot. But there's only food enough for 10 days."

Then suddenly, with a roar and a whistle, a cannonball screamed over the roof of the log house. The little building shook.

Captain Smollett said, "Oh, ho! Blaze

away, then! You have little enough powder already, my boys!"

"Captain, the log house is invisible from the ship," said the squire. "It must be the flag they're aiming at. Would it be wiser to take it down?"

Captain Smollett said, "Take down the British flag? No, sir—not I." As soon as he said it, the rest of the men agreed with him.

All through the evening the cannon thundered away. But ball after ball flew short, or harmlessly kicked up the sand inside the stockade.

Later that evening, a noise was heard outside the log house. Standing guard outside the door, Hunter said, "Listen! Someone is calling to us."

A small voice cried, "Doctor! Squire Trelawney! It's me—Jim Hawkins!"

§6 Clashing Cutlasses

Dr. Livesey and the others welcomed me warmly. I told them of my adventures and my meeting with Ben Gunn.

Before nightfall, we buried poor Redruth. Then we made our plans. We had very little food. Our best hope was to kill off the mutineers. From 19 men, they were already down to just 15, and two of those had been wounded. And we had two other things on our side—fever and rum.

The mutineers had broken into the rum on the *Hispaniola.* We could hear them roaring and singing late into the night. As for fever, Dr. Livesey bet his wig that, without medicine, half of them would be on their backs in a week.

I was dreadful tired that night, and slept like a dead man. The next morning, I was wakened by a bustle and the sound of voices.

I heard someone say, "Look, a flag of truce! It's Long John Silver himself!"

Captain Smollett ordered, "Stay indoors, men. I'll bet ten to one this is a trick."

Then the captain called out to Long John Silver: "What's the meaning of your flag of truce?"

Long John Silver cried out, "It's Captain Silver, sir—come to make a deal with you."

"I don't know any *Captain* Silver. Who might he be?" Smollett answered.

Long John Silver said, "That's *me*, sir! These poor men have chosen me captain— since you deserted, sir."

"I don't have the least desire to talk to you," Smollett said. "If you wish to talk to me, come here. But if you pull any tricks, the Lord help you."

Long John Silver said in a cheerful voice, "The word of a gentleman is good enough for me, Captain Smollett."

Long John Silver threw his crutch over the stockade fence. Then, with great energy and skill, he pulled himself up and over the fence and sat down in the sand.

"So here you are," Captain Smollett said. "If you have anything to say, say it quickly."

"Well now, look here," said Silver. "That was a pretty good trick of yours last night. One of you was right busy with the hand spike. Maybe it shook up the men a little. Maybe I was shook myself. Maybe that's why I'm here to offer you a deal."

Captain Smollett was cool as could be. He said, "Well?"

Silver's words were a riddle to Captain Smollett. But you would never have guessed it from his tone. As for me, I had a feeling Ben Gunn had paid the mutineers a visit last night. So now we had only *14* enemies to deal with!

Long John Silver said, "Well, here it is— you give us the map to the treasure, and we'll divide it with you, man for man. Then we'll offer you a choice. You can come back on the *Hispaniola* with us, and I'll put you safe on shore somewhere. Or maybe that ain't your fancy. After all, some of my men are rough, and have old scores to settle. So if you want, you can stay here. I give my word to speak to the first ship I see, and send 'em here to pick you up."

Captain Smollett knocked out the ashes from his pipe. He said, "Is that all, Silver? Now you'll hear me. If you and your men will come up one by one, unarmed, I'll put each of you in chains. Then I'll take you home to a fair trial in England. If you won't, I'll see all of you in Davey Jones's locker. Now be off, and double quick."

Long John Silver cried, "You'll at least give me a hand up!"

Captain Smollett said, "Not I."

Long John Silver crawled along the sand, swearing. When he reached the log house, he got hold of it and pulled himself up on his crutch. Then he spat into our spring! "There!" he cried. *"That's* what I think of ye! Before the hour is up, you'll not be laughing. Them that *die* will be the *lucky* ones!"

With a last awful curse, off he went.

We got our weapons ready. The sun climbed over the trees. Soon the sand seemed to be baking. We stood waiting in a fever of heat and worry. An hour passed.

Suddenly Joyce whipped up his musket and fired. In answer, the mutineers fired shots from every direction. Several bullets hit the log house, but not one entered.

Then, with a loud scream, a band of mutineers ran straight for the stockade. A rifle ball sang through the doorway and blew the doctor's musket to bits.

Like monkeys, the mutineers swarmed over the fence. Squire Trelawney and Abraham Gray fired again and again. Three mutineers fell. The four that were left ran straight for us.

One of the mutineers, Job Anderson, roared, "At 'em, mates!"

Another mutineer grabbed Hunter's musket from his hands and hit him in the head with all his might. Poor Hunter fell to the floor like a bag of potatoes.

The log house was full of smoke from our gunfire. There was a lot of yelling and confusion, and bangs and flashes from pistol shots, which rang in my ears.

Captain Smollett cried, "*Out*, lads! Fight

'em in the open! Cutlasses!"

I snatched a cutlass from the pile. Someone else snatched another just then and gave me a cut across the knuckles, which I hardly felt. I dashed out the door and saw Dr. Livesey chasing a mutineer down the hill. With a great slash, he sent the man sprawling on his back.

Captain Smollett cried, "Get around the house, lads!"

I followed his order. Next moment I was face to face with Job Anderson. Bellowing like a bull, he raised his cutlass. It flashed in the sunlight. I leaped to one side and saw Abraham Gray coming up behind me. He cut down Job Anderson before the man could raise his cutlass again.

Dr. Livesey cried, "Get into the log house, lads! Fire from the house!"

But no one listened to him. For suddenly, the mutineers were climbing over the fence and running away. Dr. Livesey, Abraham Gray, and I then ran back to the log house. We saw the price we had paid for victory. Hunter lay without moving. Joyce had taken a shot to the head—he was gone. In the middle of the room, Squire Trelawney was holding the captain. One man was as pale as the other.

Captain Smollett said, "Have they run?"

"All that could," said Dr. Livesey. "But there's five of them will never run again."

"*Five!*" Smollett said weakly. "That's better. So now we're four to nine. That's better odds than we had at the start."

We did what we could for Hunter. But he never came to again. As for Captain

Smollett, one of Job Anderson's bullets had broken his shoulderblade and touched the lung. The second bullet had torn some muscles in his calf. He was sure to recover, but for some weeks he would not be able to walk or move his arm.

My own cut across the knuckles was a flea bite. Dr. Livesey patched it with plaster and pulled my ears in the bargain.

After dinner, Squire Trelawney and Dr. Livesey sat talking. Then Dr. Livesey took up his hat and pistols. Putting the map in his pocket, he set off into the woods. I had a feeling he must be going off to find Ben Gunn.

As soon as he left, an idea came to me. When no one was watching, I filled my pockets with biscuits and took pistols, powder, and bullets.

My plan was to find Ben Gunn's boat. I was sure the men would not let me go alone, so I decided to slip out when no one was watching. I knew this was wrong. With me gone, there would be one less to guard the log house. But I was only a boy at the time, and I had made up my mind.

§7 Jim on His Own

I found Ben Gunn's boat near the white rock he had spoken of. Hidden deep in the bushes, it was a rough-looking thing, made of raw wood and covered with goat skin. It was very small, even for me, but light and easy to carry.

Now that I had found the boat, I had another idea. This was to slip out at night and cut the *Hispaniola* loose from her anchor. If she drifted up to the island, the mutineers, after the fierce fight this morning, might take off to sea. I wanted to stop them if I could.

As night came on, fog clouded the sky. I could see but two points of light. One was the fire of the mutineers, who were camped in the swampy area of the island. Another was a dim light in the cabin of the *Hispaniola*.

I waded out and set Ben's boat in the direction of our ship. She was a safe little craft, but difficult to manage. She turned in every direction except the one I wanted. Luckily, the tide was in my favor.

I soon reached the *Hispaniola,* and began to cut the rope that held her anchor. Above me I could hear the angry voices of two mutineers. One voice I knew—it belonged to Israel Hands.

I had cut the rope almost through. Then curiosity got the better of me. I climbed up the side of the ship to the cabin window. Beneath the smoky lamp, I saw the furious faces of Israel Hands and another mutineer. The men were locked in a deadly struggle. Each man had a hand on the other's throat.

I dropped back down to my little boat and cut the rope to the *Hispaniola*'s anchor. At once the night wind began taking the *Hispaniola* toward Treasure Island. The wind and current took my little boat, too— and I could do nothing to stop her. I was afraid I might drift into some dangerous breakers.

I lay down in the bottom of the little boat and prayed. I must have stayed there for hours, expecting death with each new wave that sprayed over me. Finally, I grew so tired that I fell asleep. I dreamed of home and the old Admiral Benbow Inn.

It was broad day when I awoke. I found myself tossing at the south end of Treasure Island. The waves were great, smooth swells. My little boat skimmed over them as lightly as a bird. I paddled carefully, mostly letting the boat have its way. Little by little, I drew closer to shore. I longed to be on land again, for I was tortured by thirst.

Then the current swept me past a point of land and I saw the *Hispaniola*. She was less than a half-mile away!

Coming closer, I saw her sails going back and forth, shivering in the wind. It was plain that no one was steering her! I wondered where the mutineers were. Either they were dead drunk, or they had deserted her. I thought that if I could get on board, I might return her to Captain Smollett.

I came as close to the *Hispaniola* as I

could. Then I sprang to my feet and leaped, swamping my little boat underwater. As I grabbed onto the ship I heard a dull thump. I knew that the *Hispaniola* had put an end to old Ben's boat. Now I was left on the great ship with no retreat.

The two men were on deck, sure enough. One man was dead on his back. His teeth showed through his open lips. The other man was Israel Hands. He gave out a low moan, which went right to my heart. But when I remembered the talk I had heard from the apple barrel, all pity left me.

I leaned close to Israel Hands. All he could say was, "Brandy."

I went downstairs to the cabin. The floor was thick with mud. Empty bottles clinked with the rolling of the ship. I found a bottle with some brandy left in it. For myself I got some biscuits, a great handful of raisins, and a small piece of cheese. Then I had a good, deep drink of water.

I gave Israel Hands the brandy. "I've come on board to take charge of this ship, Mr. Hands," I told him. "You'll look to me as your captain until further notice."

He gave me a sour look, but said nothing. I went on, "By-the-by, Mr. Hands, this flag won't do. Better to have no flag than this."

With that, I pulled down the Jolly Roger and chucked it overboard.

Israel Hands watched me closely and slyly. "Now, Captain Hawkins," he said, "you'll be wanting to get on shore. You ain't the man to sail this ship, I guess. If you gives me food and drink, and tie up my wound, I'll tell you how to sail her."

We struck our bargain on the spot. I used my mother's silk handkerchief to tie up the man's stab wound. Then, in three minutes, I had the *Hispaniola* sailing easily before the wind along the coast of Treasure Island.

After our next meal, Israel Hands said, "Get me a bottle of wine, Jim. This brandy's too strong for my head."

I did not believe Israel Hands wanted brandy instead of wine. He wanted me to leave the deck—that much was plain.

I went down below as noisily as I could. Then I slipped out of my shoes and sneaked back to watch him. On his hands and knees, he crawled across the deck. Then he reached into a coil of rope and pulled out a long knife. He tucked it into his jacket.

This was all I needed to know. Israel Hands could move about—and he was armed! Yet I could trust him on one point. We needed each other to get the boat on shore.

I brought him back some wine. Taking a long drink, he said, "The tide's good by now. Just take my orders, Captain Hawkins, and we'll sail in and be done with it."

We sailed the *Hispaniola* into a narrow inlet. I had easily learned how to handle the tiller—Israel Hands was an excellent teacher. But as we came near to the beach, his directions were many and fast. I forgot to keep a close watch on him.

Just as I was waiting to feel the ship touch the sand, something made me turn my head. There was Israel Hands, coming at me with the knife in his hand! Before he could reach me, I leaped sideways, letting go of the tiller. It struck him across the chest.

I jumped out of the way, drew my pistol,

and fired. But nothing happened! The pistol was soaked with seawater!

I climbed up the mast as fast as I could. There I lost no time in getting my pistol ready with dry powder.

Israel Hands began to see the dice rolling against him. He put the knife between his teeth and started to slowly climb up the mast. But by then I was ready.

I pointed the pistol at his face. "One more step, Mr. Hands, and I'll blow your brains out!" I cried.

Suddenly, something shot toward me like an arrow. I felt a sharp pang, and there I was—pinned by the shoulder to the mast! Then both my pistols went off and fell from my hands! But they did not fall alone. With a choked cry, Israel Hands let go of the sail and plunged headfirst into the water.

8 Pieces of Eight!

Israel Hands lay on the sand in the clear, green water. The sight of him made me feel sick, faint, and terrified. I had a horror of falling into the water beside him! Holding tight to the mast, I shut my eyes until my mind became clear again, and my racing heart grew quiet.

I found that the knife held me by a near pinch of skin. It came out easily. The wound pained me a great deal, and bled freely. But it was neither deep nor dangerous.

The sun was near to setting. I cut down the sails so the *Hispaniola* would not drift. Then I set off for the stockade. In spite of the pain, I wanted nothing more than to boast of what I had done.

As I came near the stockade I was surprised to see the light of a large bonfire.

Captain Smollett had always been careful of firewood. As I drew closer, I heard the sound of snoring. No one was keeping watch! I blamed myself for leaving with so few men to stand guard.

By this time I had reached the door of the log house. Walking in, I looked forward to seeing their faces when they found me there in the morning.

All of a sudden, a familiar shrill voice rang out. "Pieces of eight! Pieces of eight! Pieces of eight!"

It was Silver's parrot! I turned to run, but fell into two strong arms that held me tight.

Long John Silver cried out, "Bring a torch, Dick!"

The torch was brought. Looking around, my heart filled with black despair. The mutineers had the house and food! I could only guess that my friends were dead.

Long John Silver sat down and began to fill his pipe. "So, here's Jim Hawkins who's dropped in," he said. "Since you're here, I'll give you a piece of my mind. I've always liked you, Jim. You're a lad of spirit.

I always wanted you to join up with me, and now you'll have to. Your friends have gone against you."

So far so good. I only believed about half of what Long John Silver said. But at least my friends were still alive.

"If I'm to join with you," I said, "I have a right to know what's what, and where my friends are."

"All right," he said. "Dr. Livesey came yesterday with a flag of truce and a bargain. So we bargained, and here we are—house, brandy, firewood, and food. As for them, I don't know where they went."

I said, "I'm not such a fool. There's a thing or two I must tell *you*. Here you are, in a bad way—ship lost, treasure lost, men lost. If you want to know who did it, it was I! I was in the apple barrel the night we sighted land. I heard every word you said. As for the *Hispaniola,* it was *I* who cut her free from her anchor. I killed the men you left on board, and I brought her where you'll never see her again. I've had the top of this business from the first. I no more fear you than I fear a fly! Kill me, if you please, or spare me. But if you spare me, I'll save you from the gallows. When you fellows are in court for piracy, I'll save you all I can. It's for you to choose."

Tom Morgan sprang up and thrust his knife at me. "Then here goes!" he said.

Long John Silver cried out angrily, "Avast there, Tom Morgan! Did you think *you* was captain here?"

Another man said, "Tom's right."

The men murmured among themselves.

"Did any of you gentlemen want to have it out with me?" asked Silver. "Well, I'm ready. Take a cutlass, him that dares. And I'll see the color of his insides!"

Not a man answered.

The men stepped back and whispered to each other. Then one stepped forward. He was a sick-looking fellow, with yellow eyes. He said, "Asking your pardon, sir. I claim my right to step outside for a council."

One by one, the men disappeared out the door. Long John Silver and I were left alone.

"Jim Hawkins," he whispered, "they could throw me over. Then they'll torture and kill you. I'm your last card, Jim, and you're mine! I'll save your life if I can. And you can keep Long John Silver from hanging.

"There's trouble coming, for sure," he went on. "Now tell me something, Jim. Why did Dr. Livesey give me the treasure map?"

My face showed such surprise that he asked no more questions.

"Ah, well, he did," Silver continued. "Dr. Livesey must have had his reasons for giving it to me—bad or good."

61

The mutineers soon came back inside. One of them handed a small piece of paper to Long John Silver.

Long John Silver looked at the paper and said, *"The Black Spot!* I thought so. Why, you've gone and cut this paper out of a Bible. What fool has cut a Bible?"

One of the mutineers said, "It was Dick."

Long John Silver said, "Dick, was it? Well, Dick can start saying his prayers."

But then George Merry, the man with the yellow eyes, said, "Belay that talk, Long John Silver! You don't fool this crew no more. You've made a hash of the cruise. You let the enemy out of this here trap for nothing. And then, how about this boy?"

"I made a hash of this cruise, did I?" Long John Silver said quietly. "You know my plan. If you'd have listened to me, we'd be on the *Hispaniola* this very night—and the treasure in her hold, by thunder! But who crossed me? Why, it was *you* fools! As for the boy, isn't he a hostage? Why, he might be our last chance!

"And you ask about the bargain I made

with the enemy? First of all, I bargained for the doctor. What about you, George Merry? You with eyes the color of lemon peel from the fever? Is it worth nothing to have a real college doctor come to see you every morning? And look here—here's something else I bargained for—and won!"

At that, he threw down the treasure map.

The mutineers leaped on it like cats on a mouse. They quickly passed it from hand to hand. Laughing like children, the men shouted and swore in delight.

One of the mutineers said, "Yes, that's Captain Flint's writing, for sure."

"So it is," said Silver. "Well, how say you, men? Now you can choose who you please for captain."

The mutineers cried, "Long John Silver for captain! Long John Silver forever!"

§9 The Treasure Hunt

That was the end of the night's business. Soon after, we lay down to sleep. It was a long time before I could close an eye. I wondered what would become of me. I also thought about Long John Silver, and the remarkable game he was playing. On the one hand, he was keeping all the mutineers together. On the other hand, he was trying to save his own life.

The next morning we were awakened by a call. "Ahoy! Here's the doctor!"

And it was. I was glad he was here. But I felt ashamed to look him in the face.

Dr. Livesey checked on his patients. One mutineer had a wound from a fight. Others, like George Merry, needed medicine for malaria. At last Dr. Livesey said, "Now I should like to have a talk with Jim Hawkins."

"No!" George Merry thundered.

Long John Silver roared, "Silence!" Then he turned to me and said, "I'll have Dr. Livesey step just outside the stockade. You, Jim, can talk to him through the fence. Will you give me your word of honor that you'll not run off?"

I promised.

The mutineers were angry. They accused Long John Silver of trying to make a separate peace with the enemy, while doing nothing for them. And, of course, this was exactly what he was doing. I could not imagine how Silver could keep his men from rising up against him. But he was twice the man they were, and he had gotten the treasure map for them.

Dr. Livesey walked outside the stockade fence. Long John Silver took me to him. "Jim Hawkins here will tell you how I saved his life," he said. "Maybe you'll remember that, doctor." Then he left us alone.

Dr. Livesey turned to me. He said sadly, "Well, Jim, you didn't dare run off when Captain Smollett was well. But when he couldn't stop you, you left. It was downright cowardly, Jim!"

Beginning to cry, I said, "Doctor, you might spare me, for my life hangs by a thread. But if they torture me—"

Looking pained, Dr. Livesey interrupted. He said, "Jim, I can't have this! Jump over, and we'll run for it."

I said, "No sir, you know right well *you* wouldn't run away yourself! But listen, Doctor, first I must tell you where the ship is. She lies in the North Inlet."

Dr. Livesey cried, "The *ship*?"

I told Dr. Livesey of my adventures. He listened in silence.

"There is a kind of fate in this," he said at last. "Every step, it's you that saves our lives. For one thing, you found Ben Gunn. That was the best thing you ever did."

Then Dr. Livesey turned to Long John Silver, who was standing not far away. He said quietly, "Long John Silver, I'll give you some advice. Don't be in any great hurry to find the treasure. Keep the boy close to you, and when you need help, call. And I'll tell you something more. If we both get out of this trap alive, I'll do my best to save you."

Long John Silver's face shone. He said, "You couldn't say more, sir. Not if you was my mother."

Dr. Livesey shook hands with me through the fence. Then he nodded to Long John Silver and set off quickly into the woods.

When Long John Silver and I were alone, he turned to me. He said, "Jim, if I saved your life, you saved mine—and I'll not forget it. I seen the doctor waving you to run for it. And I seen you saying no, as plain as if I'd heard it. And now, Jim, we're to go treasure hunting. We'll save our necks in spite of fate and fortune."

But when we joined the mutineers for breakfast, Long John Silver said to them, "We'll take our hostage here, Jim Hawkins, on our treasure hunt. He might be handy in case of accidents—until we get the treasure and we're back on the ship. Then we'll give Jim Hawkins his share, to be sure, for all his kindness."

The men were in good humor now, but I

felt downcast. If Long John Silver stayed loyal to the mutineers, money and freedom might be his. If he chose to be loyal to Dr. Livesey and the others, the best he could hope for was a bare escape from hanging.

Soon after breakfast we set off with the treasure map. The men were armed to the teeth. Some carried picks and shovels, too. I had a rope tied around my waist. Long John Silver held the end of the rope in one hand, or between his powerful teeth.

The treasure map was marked with an "X," but it was hard to recognize the place exactly. On the map, the closest thing to the "X" was a tall tree. It lay on a plateau between Spyglass Hill and Mizzenmast Hill. The exact spot could only be found by reading the compass.

We rowed the mutineers' two boats to a distant beach. Then we began to climb up the tall plateau between Spyglass and Mizzenmast Hill. Long John Silver and I lagged behind the rest. Strong as he was, he often needed my help with his one leg and his crutch.

We had almost reached the top when one man gave a fearful cry.

"He can't have found the treasure," said Silver, "for that's at the top."

When we reached the spot, we saw it—it was a human skeleton, with just a few shreds of clothing on it.

George Merry said, "He was a seaman. At least, this is good sea cloth."

"Why are his bones lying like that?" Long John Silver said. "It ain't natural."

Indeed, the skeleton lay with its hands raised over its head, like a diver's.

"I've got an idea in my old brain," Long John Silver said. "Let's look at this here compass." It was just as Silver suspected. The skeleton pointed straight toward the "X" on the treasure map.

Long John Silver laughed. "I thought so. This is one of Flint's jokes, make no mistake. He killed them six men, and this one he hauled here and laid down in line by compass."

One of the men looked around nervously. "If ever a spirit walked, it would be Flint's.

That old Captain Flint died bad, he did."

Long John Silver said, "Come, come! Stow this talk. Flint's dead, and he don't walk. At least, he won't walk by day. Let's go ahead for the treasure."

We walked on. The mutineers' voices got lower and lower. Then all of a sudden, out of the trees in front of us, a thin, high voice began to sing:

"Fifteen men on the dead man's chest —
Yo-ho-ho, and a bottle of rum!"

The men's faces went white.

George Merry cried, "It's Flint!"

The song stopped as suddenly as it began.

Long John Silver said, "This won't do, men. It's someone having a joke. That voice is flesh and blood." But his lips were white.

The same voice then broke out again from the trees. It called, "Bring the rum, Darby McGraw! Bring the rum!"

One of the men cried out, "Why, those was Flint's last words!"

"That fixes it!" another man said. "Let's get out of here!"

Yet another man took out his Bible and started praying. But Long John Silver could not be stopped. "Shipmates," he said, "I'm here to get that treasure—and I'll not be beat by man nor devil! I was never afraid of Captain Flint in his life, and, by thunder, I'm not afraid to face him dead!"

"Belay there, Long John Silver," George Merry said. "Don't you cross a spirit."

"Spirit?" said Long John Silver. "Well, maybe. But there's one thing not clear to me. I heard an echo. Now, what's a spirit doing with an echo?"

The men were greatly relieved. George Merry said, "Well, that's so. You've a head on your shoulders, Long John Silver, and no mistake. And come to think of it, that was a bit like Flint's voice, but it was *more* like somebody's else's. It was like—"

Long John Silver cried, "Ben Gunn!"

Tom Morgan said, "Aye, Ben Gunn!"

"Why, nobody minds Ben Gunn," George Merry cried. "Dead *or* alive!"

The color returned to the men's faces. They took up their tools and went on.

We could see the tall tree rising in the distance. Now that their fear was past, the men's thoughts turned to the treasure that lay somewhere beneath that tree—*seven hundred thousand pounds in gold!* The mutineers' eyes burned in their heads. Their very souls were bound up in that fortune. A whole lifetime of spending and pleasure lay ahead for each of them.

Long John Silver hurried forward. He plucked furiously at the rope that held me to him. From time to time he gave me a deadly look. I feared that with the treasure so near, his promise and Dr. Livesey's warning were things of the past.

The mutineers broke into a run.

Then suddenly, we saw them all stop. A low cry arose. Long John Silver rushed ahead. Then we too came to a stop.

Before us lay a great, empty pit. The treasure had been found and stolen. The seven hundred thousand pounds was gone!

§10 Ben Gunn's Secret

Long John Silver passed me a double-barreled pistol. He whispered, "Jim, stand by for trouble."

Now he was quite friendly to me. I could not help whispering back, "So, Silver, you've changed sides again?"

There was no time for him to answer. With curses and cries the men leaped into the pit. Tom Morgan found a single piece of gold. He held it up in scorn.

George Merry screamed at Long John Silver, "So *this* is your seven hundred thousand pounds, is it?"

In a fury the men scrambled out of the pit. The five of them stood on one side of the pit while Long John Silver and I were on the other.

George Merry said, "There's only two of

them. One's an old cripple and the other's a cub that I mean to have the heart of!"

As he raised his knife, *crack! crack! crack!*—three musket shots flashed out of the bushes. George Merry tumbled headfirst into the pit. Another man fell dead on his side. The other three turned and ran.

Dr. Livesey, Abraham Gray, and Ben Gunn ran up, their muskets smoking. Seeing the mutineers run toward Mizzenmast Hill, we set off toward the mutineers' boats on the beach. As we walked, Dr. Livesey told

Long John Silver and me about all that had happened while I was held captive.

On the morning the mutineers had attacked the stockade, Dr. Livesey had gone to see Ben Gunn. He learned Ben's secret: Long ago, Ben Gunn had dug up the treasure and hauled it, little by little, to his cave.

Then Dr. Livesey made his bargain with the mutineers. In exchange for the map, which was now useless, the mutineers let them leave the stockade without firing on them. This way, Dr. Livesey and the others could get away from the swampy area, where they risked catching the fever. And they could also keep a guard on the money.

The doctor knew I would be in danger when the treasure was found missing. So he, Abraham Gray, and Ben Gunn started out for the tall tree to intercept the mutineers. But Dr. Livesey was afraid we might reach the tall tree before he did. So he sent Ben Gunn, the fastest runner, to do his best alone. And Ben Gunn did a very good job indeed. By playing on the men's superstitions, he frightened them and slowed their journey.

By this time we had reached the mutineers' boats. We broke up one boat with an axe. Then we got on board the other and rowed quickly to the North Inlet. The *Hispaniola* was there, drifting about just inside the inlet. Either the last tide or a strong wind had set her floating free.

We sailed the little boat around to Rum Cove, the nearest point to Ben Gunn's cave. Squire Trelawney met us near the beach. To me he was kind, but when Long John Silver greeted him, his face turned red.

"Long John Silver," said the squire, "you're a villain and an impostor. I am told I must not prosecute you. Well, then, I will not. But the dead men, sir, hang around your neck like stones."

Long John Silver said, "Thank you kindly, sir."

Squire Trelawney said, "Don't you dare thank me! Stand back!"

We all went into the cave. It was a large, roomy place, with a floor of sand. Captain Smollett lay resting before a big fire. At the back of the cave, I saw great heaps of coins and bars of gold—Flint's treasure! It had cost the lives of 17 brave men from the *Hispaniola.*

Perhaps no man alive could tell how many lives had been lost in collecting that money. Who knew how many good ships had been made to sink, or how many brave men made to walk the plank? Who knew what shame and lies and cruelty had been caused by this treasure?

The next morning we fell to work, bringing the treasure to the *Hispaniola.* With one man standing guard, the three mutineers who were left did not bother us. Abraham Gray and Ben Gunn came and went with the boat. The rest of us piled treasure on the beach for them to row to the *Hispaniola.* It was slow work. The men would tie two gold bars to a piece of rope, and pull it from the cave to the beach. I was kept busy in the cave, packing the coins into bread bags.

Day after day this work went on. We saw nothing of the last three mutineers until we were finished. We had decided to leave them on the island. We left them powder and bullets for hunting, tools, a few medicines, some rope, clothes, and tobacco.

Then one fine morning, we finally left Treasure Island. As we began to sail past the southern point, we saw the mutineers on the beach. They called out to us to have mercy, and not leave them to die in such a place. It went to our hearts to leave them that way—but we could not risk another mutiny. And to take them home to the hangman's noose would have been a cruel sort of kindness.

When it was clear that we would not stop for them, one of the mutineers let out an angry cry. He whipped his musket to his shoulder and sent a shot whistling over Long John Silver's head.

We were short of men, so we set sail for the nearest port in Spanish America. There we dropped anchor in a beautiful gulf. As soon as we stepped off the *Hispaniola,* we were surrounded with smiling faces of people selling fruits and vegetables. It was a charming contrast to our dark and bloody stay on Treasure Island.

That night we visited with the captain of

an English man-of-war. When we returned to the *Hispaniola,* we learned that Long John Silver was gone. He had slipped away with one of the sacks of gold.

I think we were all glad to be rid of him so easily.

Well, to make a long story short, once we got a few new hands on board, we made a good trip home. Only five of the men who set out on the *Hispaniola* returned with her.

All of us had a large share of the treasure. Each man used it wisely or foolishly, according to his nature. Captain Smollett is now retired from the sea. Abraham Gray not only saved his money, but is part owner of a fine ship. As for Ben Gunn, he spent or lost his money in 19 days. He was given a lodge to keep, where he still lives.

Of Long John Silver we have heard no more. But still in my worst dreams I hear the booming of the waves around Treasure Island, or the sharp voice of Long John Silver's parrot crying, "Pieces of eight! Pieces of eight!"